This book belongs to

....

Written by Tim Bugbird.
Illustrated by Lara Ede.
Designed by Annie Simpson and Sarah Vince.

Annie the Apple Pie Fairy

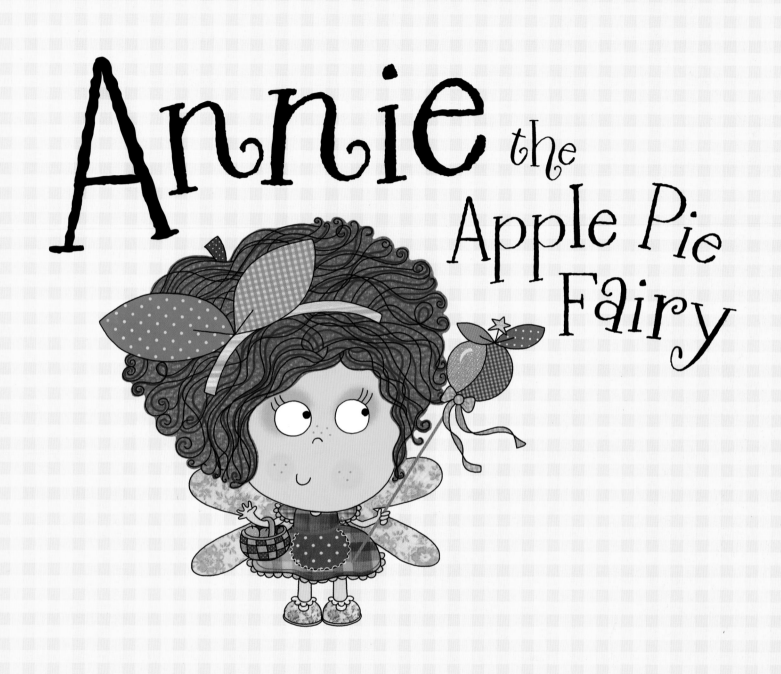

Tim Bugbird · Lara Ede

make
believe
ideas

Once in a wood, by a bubbling brook,
up high in an old apple tree,
lived a fairy named Annie, a famous cook,
who baked apple pies on TV!

She had her own show
for years and years,
with her best friends,
Pip and Cora.

Every show ended with
whoops and **cheers** –
the fairies simply **adored** her!

All Annie's pies were made with care, simply, and with nothing wasted.

Whether with berries, or pecans and pears, they were the best you've ever tasted!

Then one day the TV screens
turned a little **glary**.
In a **blaze** of **color**, a new face appeared:

Sondra the Strudel Fairy!

Sondra's style was **fancy** –
her pies were **never** plain.

The fairies switched to Sondra's show,
time and **time** again!

Pip declared, "Chef Sondra
will **beat** us if we let her.

So we **must** do what Sondra does.

But do it **much, much better!**"

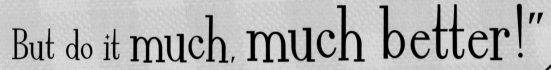

"Sondra **thinks** that she's the **tops**," said Cora with a frown.

"We'll have to pull out **all the stops** to **win** back your **baking crown**!"

And so, between the TV chefs, there arose a competition: to make *fancy pies* and be **the best** became each fairy's mission.

Every pie the rivals made was **fab-ul-ous-ly** fashioned, with **toppings** and **twirls** so high they swayed – decoration was **never** rationed!

Fancy Pies

Inside Annie's and Sondra's **homes,**
the sound you always heard
was the **clatter**
and **clunk** of gadgets,
which became ever more
absurd!

They had machines for
cutting, **slicing,**
peeling, *dicing,*
flaking, shaking,
beating, and **breaking,**
rolling, molding,
chopping, folding,
whipping, mixing,
brushing, and **fixing!**

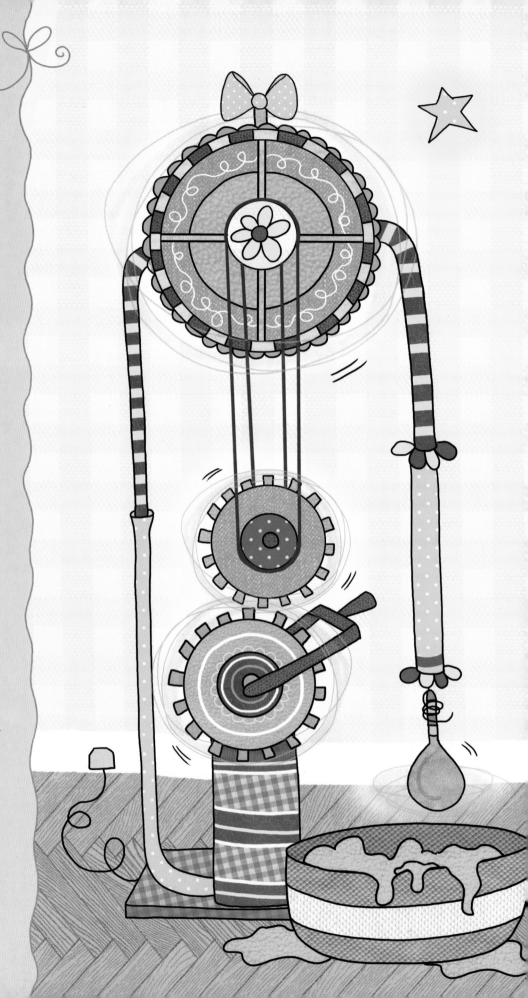

eggs

butter

flour

Soon **every** fairy across the land was following **Sondra's** trend.
Bigger, better, never bland – wherever would it **end?**

The machines made every kind of thing, in every shape and size.

But nobody seemed to notice – not one made apple pies.

But still the gadgets **pinged** and **popped**, with **whirs** and **purrs** and **clangs**, until the night when everything **stopped**, with a **flash** and a deafening . . . .

The fairies had a big surprise –
their power had totally blown!

Feeling scared, they took to the skies,
and flocked to Annie's tree home.

Pip found **candles** to light the scene and **slippers** to warm their feet, but with **nothing** to power their cooking machines, what would the **poor** fairies **eat**?

Candles

Cora **peered** inside the pantry.
Annie joined her in **despair**.
As far as either one could **see**,
there was next to **nothing** there!
Just **apples** . . .
and **butter** . . .
and **sugar** . . .
and **flour**.

Annie **sighed** and said to Sondra,
"I think things got out of hand.
We **forgot** what **matters** in the end,
we just **didn't** understand."

flour

"Now I know what we should do:
we must bake an apple pie.
We'll add a spoonful of loving –
the ingredient money can't buy."

The **pie** was made the **old-fashioned** way,
tasting **sweet**, just as it should.

Sondra said: "Let's not compete," and **apple pie** was back for **good!**

Annie and Sondra worked together and saw their friendship grow

as they starred with Pip and Cora on their brand-new TV show!